The Ghosts Go Scaring

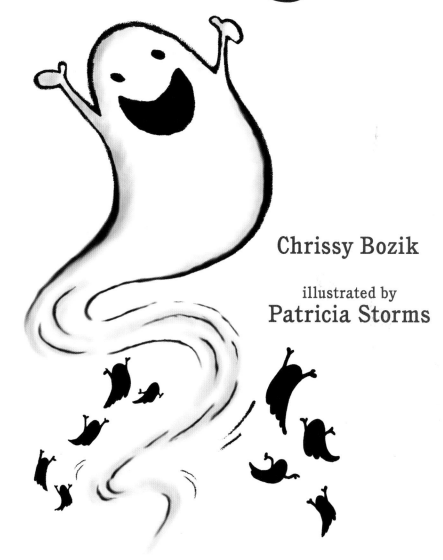

Chrissy Bozik

illustrated by
Patricia Storms

Sky Pony Press
New York

First published by Scholastic Canada Ltd. as The Ghosts Go Spooking, 2015
First Sky Pony Press edition, 2016

Sky Pony Press books may be purchased in bulk at special discounts for sales promotion, corporate gifts, fund-raising, or educational purposes. Special editions can also be created to specifications. For details, contact the Special Sales Department, Sky Pony Press, 307 West 36th Street, 11th Floor, New York, NY 10018 or info@skyhorsepublishing.com.

Sky Pony® is a registered trademark of Skyhorse Publishing, Inc.®, a Delaware corporation.

Visit our website at www.skyponypress.com.

10 9 8 7 6 5 4 3 2 1

Manufactured in China, May 2016
This product conforms to CPSIA 2008

Library of Congress Cataloging-in-Publication Data is available on file.

ISBN: 978-1-5107-1228-7
Ebook ISBN: 978-1-5107-1229-4

The ghosts go scaring one by one,
  hurrah, hurrah!
The ghosts go scaring one by one,
  hurrah, hurrah!
The ghosts go scaring one by one,
  the little one stops to have some fun.

And they all go scaring
out in the night,
to cause a big fright.
Boo! Boo! Boo!

The ghosts go scaring two by two,
  hurrah, hurrah!
The ghosts go scaring two by two,
  hurrah, hurrah!
The ghosts go scaring two by two,
the scary one stops to shout out, "Boo!"
And they all go scaring
out in the night,
to cause a big fright.
  Boo! Boo! Boo!

Boo!

Eeek!

The ghosts go scaring three by three,
  hurrah, hurrah!
The ghosts go scaring three by three,
  hurrah, hurrah!
The ghosts go scaring three by three,
the silly one stops to wink at me.
And they all go scaring
out in the night,
to cause a big fright.
  Boo! Boo! Boo!

The ghosts go scaring four by four,
  hurrah, hurrah!
The ghosts go scaring four by four,
  hurrah, hurrah!
The ghosts go scaring four by four,
the brave one stops to knock on the door.
And they all go scaring
out in the night,
to cause a big fright.
  Boo! Boo! Boo!

The ghosts go scaring five by five,
　hurrah, hurrah!
The ghosts go scaring five by five,
　hurrah, hurrah!
The ghosts go scaring five by five,
the wiggly one stops to dance a jive.
And they all go scaring
out in the night,
to cause a big fright.
　Boo! Boo! Boo!

Do the bunny hop!

The ghosts go scaring six by six,
hurrah, hurrah!
The ghosts go scaring six by six,
hurrah, hurrah!
The ghosts go scaring six by six,
the clever one stops to do some tricks.
And they all go scaring
out in the night,
to cause a big fright.
Boo! Boo! Boo!

Better
than a
rabbit!

The ghosts go scaring seven by seven,
hurrah, hurrah!
The ghosts go scaring seven by seven,
hurrah, hurrah!
The ghosts go scaring seven by seven,
the crafty one stops for a carving lesson.
And they all go scaring
out in the night,
to cause a big fright.
Boo! Boo! Boo!

The ghosts go scaring eight by eight,
hurrah, hurrah!
The ghosts go scaring eight by eight,
hurrah, hurrah!

SQUEEEAK
CREEEA
CREEEA

The ghosts go scaring eight by eight,
the tricky one stops to creak the gate.
And they all go scaring
out in the night,
to cause a big fright.
  Boo! Boo! Boo!

The ghosts go scaring nine by nine,
  hurrah, hurrah!
The ghosts go scaring nine by nine,
  hurrah, hurrah!
The ghosts go scaring nine by nine,
the noisy one stops to howl and whine.
And they all go scaring
out in the night,
to cause a big fright.
  Boo! Boo! Boo!

We're here!

The ghosts go scaring ten by ten,
hurrah, hurrah!
The ghosts go scaring ten by ten,
hurrah, hurrah!
The ghosts go scaring ten by ten,
the bouncy one stops to shout, "Again!"
And they all go scaring
out in the night,
to cause a big fright.
Boo! Boo! Boo!

MAGIC GLASSES AND A
MYSTERIOUS BLUE BOOK

A special Kids Guide to Defeating COVID-19

By:

Michael C Johnson

DEDICATION

To my muse, I am who I am, because of you.
My daughters,

Deshanti, MaKayla, and MaKiah.

I appreciate and value you.
YOU made this book through me,
I give you all the credit, yet ill take all the earnings (Wink) lol. Thank you,
I LOVE Y'ALL

To Gretchen A Campbell, NONE of this would be possible without you,
you're a true fire starter. Thank you for all of your help!

To all the frontline workers: First responders, Educators, Food and
agriculture, Manufactures, Corrections workers, U.S. Postal Service
workers, Public transit workers, Grocery store workers, Transportation and
logistics, Foodservice workers, Shelter and housing, Finance, Information
technology, and communication, Energy, Media, Legal, Engineers, Water, and
wastewater.Thank you very much, for all you do!

There once were three sisters that felt stuck inside for so long,
But Covid-19 was still spreading fast, deadly, and strong.
Shanti is the oldest. She was lying on the couch snoring in her sleep,
Then there was Mums happily drawing a picture, not making a peep.

Mac loves adventures but sat on the floor as bored as could be,
They all felt stuck at home when they wanted to feel free.
Mac thought, and she thought there must be something they could do,
She was upset that Covid-19 was still around too.

Suddenly an idea popped into her head.
She remembered last night's dream!
Where a fairy showed up in her room
from a pretty rainbow-colored light
beam.
The fairy in her dream put a glowing
magic box under Mac's bed,
"The world needs you and your sisters,"
the fairy said.

Mac then said to herself, "Maybe the box is real, could it be true?"
As she ran to her room to check under her bed, her excitement grew.
She lifted the bed skirt and was shocked at what she found,
The same glowing box from her dream, sitting right there on the ground!

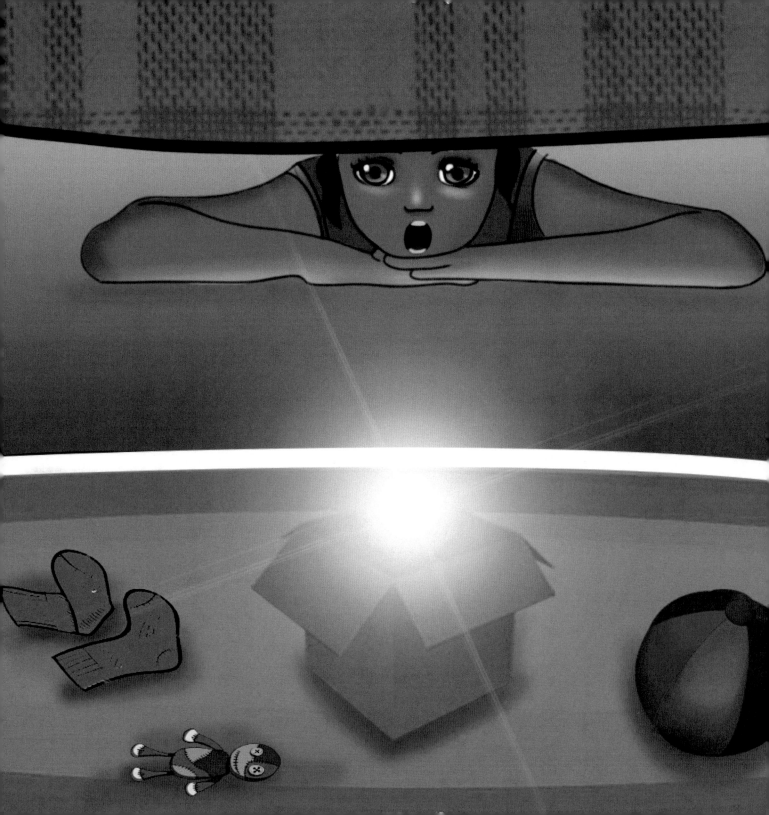

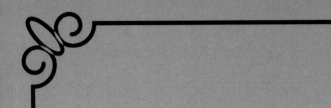

She ran as fast as she could to Mum's and woke up Shanti too.
"Hurry! Follow me. I have something to show you!"
Together they opened the magic box to have a look,
It had three pairs of sunglasses and a little blue book.

"What could it be?" Mums looked up and said,
"How to defeat Covid-19." Is what the front cover read.
The three sisters looked at each other with their eyes open wide,
Then they opened the book, and they read the guide.

Step one: Protect yourself with your favorite gloves and mask.

Step two: keep a safe distance, So the monsters won't last.

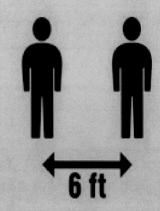

6 ft

Step three: find the big monster and defeat him fast Because he makes little monsters and Little monsters spread in a dash,
Once those are defeated, the virus will have passed.

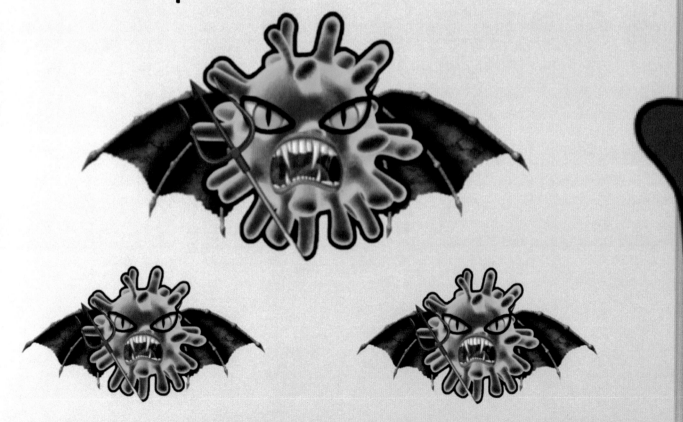

The girls searched through the book to find what to do next, When they discovered such an important part of the text.

Put on sunglasses to see the virus monsters and receive your superpowers,
You better start now. Defeating the big Virus Monster could take hours.

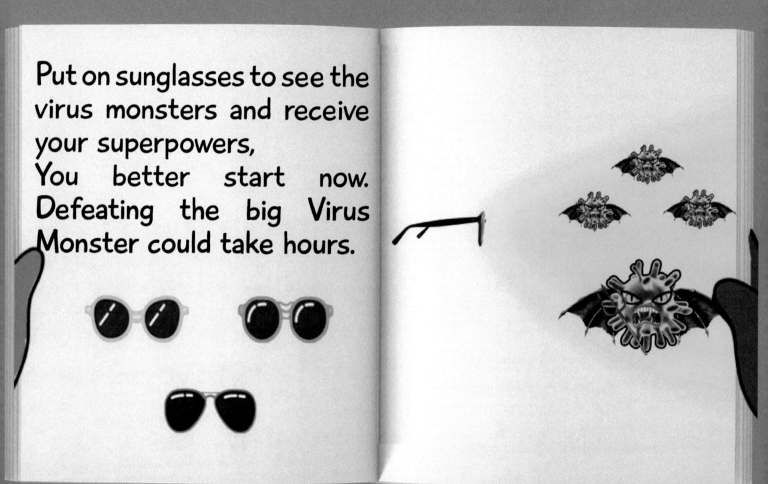

They put on their glasses and saw the little monsters everywhere!
They were shocked seeing the little green guys floating through the air.
"We have to go now!" said Shanti. It's like the girls knew what to do,
So they went outside and flew in the air, Shanti, Mac, and even Mums too.

"Where would the big Virus Monster be?" Mums asked as they flew through the sky,
Then Mac remembered seeing him in her dream. "Follow me!" was her confident reply.
They flew and they flew and finally, they arrived at the right place,
And they saw the big Virus Monster with his evil-looking face.

"Let's get him!" yelled Shanti as they prepared for a fight,
Then the Virus Monster lunged towards the girls with all of his might.
The girls have super ninja powers, so they kicked and they punched away!
Then Shanti pulled out a Super Soaker with sanitizer eliminating spray.

The virus monster saw the Super Soaker, and it suddenly got scared,
What, did he think that the sisters would come unprepared?
She squirted and squirted; the virus monster finally shrank!
"NOO!" cried the monster as he disappeared in a blink.

"YAY!" The girl's fist bump. They did what they went there to do,
And they left with a level of confidence that felt brand new.

They headed back home. Their mission didn't take long,
And there was Dad eating vegetarian pizza with pineapple in the kitchen, singing his favorite song.
Even Baby Jay was there in the kitchen too,
And she was dancing around the room with a french fry in hand like she always would do.
"Nice glasses, girls!" Dad said as they smiled because he didn't have a clue,
What to save the world, that they had to do.

There were still the little green virus monsters all around, but they couldn't defeat the rest,
That would take everyone wearing a mask, washing their hands, and all doing their best.
Mums is creative and came up with a great idea for a banner, so they made a giant one with The help of all three,
And they flew to hang it right in the city for everyone to see.

The banner was colorful and said, "We must all keep a good distance and wear our mask,
And washing our hands should be at least a 30-second task.
One thing we know with all of our hearts,
Is that we can defeat the Corona Virus if we all do our part."

People listened to the banner after they saw it from their windows or even on their morning drive,
And after soon enough, the little Covid-19 monsters wouldn't be able to survive.

THE END

Made in the USA
Columbia, SC
08 April 2021